HOW TO PLAY THE GAME?

Would You Rather questions are fun for both young and old, and a great way to open the lines of communication between family and friends.

Read the question aloud and ask everyone to give their answer and explain it further. Why did they select the option they did? Learn more about everyone playing this game.

Would You Rather questions make a great icebreaker at parties. This compact book is also a great road trip or vacation activity for kids and families to bond over.

Please note that all questions are original and this book is for entertainment purposes only. It cannot be copied or resold.

D1514754

WOULD YOU RATHER...

BE A BESTSELLING BOOK AUTHOR

~OR~

A SOLD-OUT CONCERT MUSICIAN?

BE AN UNDERCOVER DETECTIVE

~OR~

AN INTERNATIONAL SPY?

GROW A VENUS FLY TRAP

~OR~

A WORLD RECORD SIZED PUMPKIN?

WOULD YOU RATHER...

LIVE IN THE MOUNTAINS

~OR~

LIVE NEAR THE OCEAN?

WORK WITH A LARGE TEAM

~OR~

WORK BY YOURSELF?

HAVE LOTS OF QUIET NEIGHBORS

~OR~

ONE VERY NOSY NEIGHBOR?

WOULD YOU RATHER...

HAVE A FLYING MAGIC CARPET

~OR~

A DISAPPEARING SUBMARINE?

EAT UNLIMITED CHEAP PIZZA

~OR~

A SLICE OF THE WORLD'S BEST PIZZA?

BE ABLE TO DO BACKFLIPS

~OR~

BE A TALENTED BREAKDANCER?

WOULD YOU RATHER...

LIVE WHERE IT'S ALWAYS WINTER

~OR~

LIVE WHERE IT'S ALWAYS SUMMER?

YOUR WHOLE HOME IS WHITE

~OR~

EVERY WALL IS A DIFFERENT COLOR?

BE ABLE TO SPEAK WITH ANIMALS

~OR~

SPEAK ANY FOREIGN LANGUAGE?

WOULD YOU RATHER...

LIVE ON MARS

~OR~

LIVE ON THE MOON?

LIVE 24 HOURS IN ANCIENT EGYPT

~OR~

LIVE 24 HOURS IN THE WILD WEST?

BE A PENGUIN IN THE ARCTIC

~OR~

A SLOTH IN THE JUNGLE?

WOULD YOU RATHER...

HAVE MANY AVERAGE FRIENDS

~OR~

ONLY ONE TRUE BEST FRIEND?

LIVE WITHOUT TELEVISION

~OR~

LIVE WITHOUT JUNK FOOD?

BE ABLE TO BREATHE UNDERWATER

~OR~

FLY THROUGH THE AIR?

WOULD YOU RATHER...

GO TO THE DENTIST EVERY MONTH

~OR~

ONLY SWIM ONCE A YEAR?

CHANGE YOUR EYE COLOR

~OR~

CHANGE YOUR HAIR COLOR?

WEAR A UNIFORM DAILY

~OR~

HAVE TO SEW YOUR OWN CLOTHES?

WOULD YOU RATHER...

HAVE TO LAUNDER CLOTHES BY HAND

~OR~

GROW ALL YOUR OWN FOOD?

ONLY EAT CANDY FOR A DAY

~OR~

ONLY EAT POTATO CHIPS FOR A DAY?

SHOOT LICORICE FROM YOUR FINGERS

~OR~

CRY CHOCOLATE CHIP TEARS?

WOULD YOU RATHER...

HAVE TO WALK BACKWARDS

~OR~

HAVE TO SKIP & JUMP EVERYWHERE?

HAVE FEET FOR HANDS

~OR~

HAVE HANDS FOR FEET?

LIVE 80 YEARS IN THE FUTURE

~OR~

LIVE 50 YEARS IN THE PAST?

WOULD YOU RATHER...

LIVE IN A SKYSCRAPER IN NEW YORK

~OR~

LIVE ON A RANCH IN TEXAS?

ONLY EAT FOOD BEGINNING WITH "B"

~OR~

GIVE UP EATING ALL CARBS?

BE INVISIBLE TO EVERYONE

~OR~

THEY CAN SEE BUT CAN'T HEAR YOU?

WOULD YOU RATHER...

ONLY TALK 500 WORDS PER DAY

~OR~

ONLY WALK 500 STEPS PER DAY?

OWN A FLYING BROOMSTICK

~OR~

A SELF DRIVING CAR?

HAVE THE SNOW BE ICE CREAM

~OR~

HAVE THE RAIN BE APPLE JUICE?

WOULD YOU RATHER...

GROW UP WITH 12 SIBLINGS

~OR~

BE AN ONLY CHILD?

RIDE ON THE BACK OF A WOLF

~OR~

SWIM ON THE BACK OF A DOLPHIN?

BE THE MVP ON A LOSING TEAM

~OR~

BE THE WORST PLAYER ON A
WINNING TEAM?

WOULD YOU RATHER...

SWIM IN A POOL OF CHOCOLATE MILK

~OR~

SLED DOWN A HILL OF PIZZA?

WEAR YOUR PANTS BACKWARD

~OR~

WEAR SHOES ON THE WRONG FEET?

HAVE HAIR DOWN TO YOUR ANKLES

~OR~

BE COMPLETELY BALD?

WOULD YOU RATHER...

HUG A GRIZZLY BEAR

~OR~

SLEEP NEXT TO AN ALLIGATOR?

ONLY BE ABLE TO WHISPER

~OR~

ONLY BE ABLE TO SHOUT?

EAT A POUND OF RAW TOMATOES

~OR~

EAT A POUND OF RAW BROCCOLI?

WOULD YOU RATHER...

DRESS LIKE A CLOWN

~OR~

WEAR PINK BOWS IN YOUR HAIR?

GO WITHOUT WIFI FOR A YEAR

~OR~

GO WITHOUT RADIO FOR A YEAR?

EAT ONLY ONE MEAL PER DAY

~OR~

UNLIMITED CHICKEN NUGGETS?

WOULD YOU RATHER...

BE COVERED IN BEE STINGS

~OR~

A WHOLE BODY OF POISON IVY RASH?

EAT A RAW ONION

~OR~

EAT A CLOVE OF GARLIC?

HAVE LOTS OF QUIET NEIGHBORS

~OR~

ONE VERY NOSY NEIGHBOR?

WOULD YOU RATHER...

BE 2 FEET TALL

~OR~

BE 10 FEET TALL?

CLEAN HOME TOILETS EVERY DAY

~OR~

DO ALL THE DISHES EVERY DAY?

BE A BORING SUPERHERO

~OR~

BE A COOL VILLAIN?

WOULD YOU RATHER...

SING AT A PACKED KARAOKE NIGHT

~OR~

READ POETRY TO ENGLISH TEACHERS?

WEAR A PARKA IN THE DESERT

~OR~

WEAR A SWIMSUIT IN THE ARCTIC?

BE ABLE TO SPEAK EVERY LANGUAGE

~OR~

BE ABLE TO SOLVE EVERY PROBLEM?

WOULD YOU RATHER...

BUNGEE JUMP OFF A HIGH CLIFF

~OR~

BE IN A SHARK CAGE SURROUNDED?

BE THE BOSS AND WORK 12 HRS/DAY

~OR~

BE ENTRY LEVEL AND WORK 8 HRS/DAY?

HAVE A MAID TO CLEAN YOUR HOME

~OR~

A CHEF TO COOK YOUR MEALS?

WOULD YOU RATHER...

RUN ULTRA FAST

~OR~

BE SUPER STRONG?

HAVE BAD BREATH DAILY

~OR~

BE STINKY SWEATY ALL THE TIME?

HAVE A THIRD EYE

~OR~

HAVE A THIRD ARM?

WOULD YOU RATHER...

CONTROL TOMORROW'S WEATHER

~OR~

PREDICT WEATHER FOR A YEAR?

LIVE AT THE SOUTH POLE FOR A YEAR

~OR~

IN OUTER SPACE FOR A MONTH?

HAVE YOUR HOME BE ALWAYS DARK

~OR~

HAVE YOUR HOME BE ALWAYS LIGHT?

WOULD YOU RATHER...

TURN YOUR MOM INTO A UNICORN

~OR~

TURN YOUR DAD INTO A DRAGON?

HAVE A NICE TEACHER BUT LEARN NOTHING

~OR~

HAVE A MEAN TEACHER BUT LEARN A LOT?

HAVE BRIGHT PURPLE HAIR

~OR~

HAVE BRIGHT PURPLE TEETH?

WOULD YOU RATHER...

BE THE MOST POPULAR KID

~OR~

BE THE SMARTEST KID?

LIVE WITHOUT A PHONE

~OR~

LIVE WITHOUT A REFRIGERATOR?

HAVE A SONG STUCK IN YOUR HEAD

~OR~

DREAM THE SAME EVERY NIGHT?

WOULD YOU RATHER...

LIVE IN A HOUSE THAT'S TOO HOT

~OR~

LIVE IN A HOUSE THAT'S TOO COLD?

HAVE A GIRAFFE NECK

~OR~

HAVE AN ELEPHANT TRUNK?

HAVE A PET TARANTULA

~OR~

HAVE A PET PARROT WHO WON'T BE QUIET?

WOULD YOU RATHER...

HAVE A CONTINUING ITCH

~OR~

LIVE IN NONSTOP PAIN?

HAVE TO SAY EVERYTHING YOU THINK

~OR~

NOT BE ABLE TO SPEAK AT ALL?

ALWAYS WEAR EAR MUFFS

~OR~

ALWAYS WEAR NOSE PLUGS?

WOULD YOU RATHER...

PUBLISH YOUR DIARY

~OR~

MAKE A FILM OF YOUR LIFE?

COUNT GRAINS OF SAND IN SANDBOX

~OR~

COUNT CUPS OF WATER IN A POOL?

HAVE YOUR MOM SHADOW YOU FOR A MONTH

~OR~

TELL YOUR GRANDMA ALL YOUR SECRETS?

WOULD YOU RATHER...

HAVE OTHERS GOSSIP ABOUT YOU

~OR~

NOBODY TALKS ABOUT YOU AT ALL?

RUN A MARATHON WITH FRIENDS

~OR~

RUN A 1/2 MARATHON BY YOURSELF?

GET LOTS OF DAILY HOMEWORK

~OR~

GET SUPER HARD WEEKLY TESTS?

WOULD YOU RATHER...

SLEEP IN A CAVE WITH A BEAR

~OR~

HELP WRESTLE AN ALLIGATOR?

GO TO A THRILLING CIRCUS

~OR~

SEE A BORING CONCERT?

GO MOUNTAIN SNOW SKIING

~OR~

A FUN AMUSEMENT PARK?

WOULD YOU RATHER...

WALK THROUGH A HAUNTED HOUSE

~OR~

CHANGE A REALLY POOPY DIAPER?

BE A WIZARD

~OR~

BE A SUPERHERO?

FLY A KITE IN A TORNADO

~OR~

GO SURFING DURING A HURRICANE?

WOULD YOU RATHER...

ONLY BE ABLE TO CRAB WALK

~OR~

ONLY BE ABLE TO BABY CRAWL?

DIP A TACO IN CHOCOLATE SAUCE

~OR~

EAT PUMPKIN PIE WITH KETCHUP?

WORK AS DOG PARK POOPER SCOOPER

~OR~

GARBAGE COLLECTOR?

WOULD YOU RATHER...

LIVE IN A MANSION WITH MANY

~OR~

LIVE IN A SMALL APARTMENT ALONE?

HAVE 4 EARS & HEAR EVERYTHING

~OR~

HAVE 2 NOSES & SMELL EVERYTHING?

OWN EVERY TOOL IN THE WORLD

~OR~

OWN EVERY BEAUTY PRODUCT?

WOULD YOU RATHER...

SWIM LIKE A FISH

~OR~

RUN LIKE A CHEETAH?

BE WINNER OF HOME RUN CONTEST

~OR~

BE WINNER OF BEAUTY PAGEANT?

FLIP BURGERS FOR WORK & LOVE IT

~OR~

MANAGE BIG PORTFOLIOS & HATE IT?

WOULD YOU RATHER...

TAKE 1 MONTH FREE EUROPE VACAY

~OR~

TAKE 6 MONTH FREE USA VACAY?

LIVE WITHOUT EMOJIS OR ICONS

~OR~

LIVE WITHOUT TEXTING?

JUMP LIKE A KANGAROO

~OR~

FLY LIKE AN EAGLE?

WOULD YOU RATHER...

BE SUPER SMART

~OR~

BE SUPER FUNNY?

KNOW WHAT EVERYONE IS THINKING

~OR~

CHANGE HOW ONE PERSON THINKS?

CREATE A BRAND NEW TV SHOW

~OR~

WRITE A BRAND NEW HIT SONG?

WOULD YOU RATHER...

BE REALLY GOOD AT ALL SPORTS

~OR~

UNDERSTAND ALL SCIENCE?

EAT 10 ROTTEN APPLES

~OR~

EAT A COOKED SQUASH?

BECOME 5 YEARS OLDER

~OR~

BECOME 2 YEARS YOUNGER?

WOULD YOU RATHER...

WEAR A FULL SUIT OF ARMOR

~OR~

WALK AROUND NAKED?

HAVE YOUR DRAWING IN A GALLERY

~OR~

SING ONSTAGE AT A CONCERT?

FART LOUDLY IN A STORE BY MISTAKE

~OR~

GIVE A SPEECH TO 500 PEOPLE?

WOULD YOU RATHER...

BECOME A NINJA WARRIOR

~OR~

PLAY FOR A PRO FOOTBALL TEAM?

HAVE TICKETS TO YOUR FAVORITE TEAM'S BASEBALL GAME & THEY LOSE

~OR~

WATCH YOUR TEAM AT HOME ON TV & THEY WIN?

OWN ONE EXPENSIVE JEWELRY PIECE

~OR~

OWN MANY INEXPENSIVE PIECES?

WOULD YOU RATHER...

REMEMBER EVERYONE YOU'VE MET

~OR~

KNOW FUTURE PEOPLE YOU'LL MEET?

DRINK EVERY MEAL AS A SMOOTHIE

~OR~

ONLY EAT RAW FOOD?

STAR IN ONE EPISODE OF A TV SHOW

~OR~

MEET YOUR FAVORITE CELEBRITY?

WOULD YOU RATHER...

SAIL ON A YACHT

~OR~

FLY IN A HOT AIR BALLOON?

BE A CHICKEN FARMER

~OR~

WORK A FACTORY ASSEMBLY LINE?

DIP EVERY FOOD IN ROOT BEER

~OR~

ONLY EAT CAKE FOR EVERY MEAL?

WOULD YOU RATHER...

SLEEP FLOATING ON THE WATER

~OR~

SLEEP STANDING UP ALL NIGHT?

HAVE A PET TREX DINOSAUR

~OR~

HAVE A PET SLOTH?

STAY FIT WITHOUT EXERCISE OR DIET

~OR~

BECOME PRESIDENT OF THE U.S.A.?

WOULD YOU RATHER...

GO SCUBA DIVING

~OR~

GO MOUNTAIN CLIMBING?

EAT A 10 FOOT TALL ICE CREAM CONE

~OR~

EAT A 10 POUND CHOCOLATE DONUT?

BOWL A PERFECT GAME

~OR~

PITCH A NO HITTER?

WOULD YOU RATHER...

HAVE A TAIL THAT CAN'T GRAB

~OR~

HAVE WINGS THAT CAN'T FLY?

RIDE A GIANT HORSE

~OR~

RIDE A TINY MINIATURE PONY?

USE A RIDING LAWNMOWER & SHOVEL
SNOW BY HAND

~OR~

USE A PUSHMOWER FOR LAWN & A
POWERED SNOWBLOWER?

WOULD YOU RATHER...

HAVE A ROBOT TO DO EVERYTHING

~OR~

HAVE A HUMAN ASSISTANT?

HAVE A REALLY SMART BEST FRIEND

~OR~

HAVE A REALLY KIND BEST FRIEND?

PET ALL THE DOGS

~OR~

PET ALL THE CATS?

WOULD YOU RATHER...

LIVE WITHOUT FEAR

~OR~

LIVE WITHOUT LOVE?

RIDE ROLLERCOASTERS NONSTOP

~OR~

NEVER RIDE ROLLERCOASTERS AGAIN?

GROW A GIANT SUNFLOWER YOU
COULD CLIMB UP TO THE SKY

~OR~

DIG A DEEP HOLE YOU COULD CRAWL
TO THE OTHER SIDE OF THE WORLD?

WOULD YOU RATHER...

EAT A DOZEN WHOLE LEMONS

~OR~

EAT RAW SUSHI?

BLOW A GIANT BUBBLE, CLIMB IN AND FLOAT AWAY

~OR~

RIDE A MAGIC CARPET?

MEET TEN CELEBRITIES

~OR~

BE A CELEBRITY FOR A DAY?

WOULD YOU RATHER...

BE SUPER SMART WITH NO LUCK

~OR~

BE AVERAGE BUT VERY LUCKY?

BRUSH YOUR TEETH WITH SOAP

~OR~

WASH YOURSELF WITH TOOTHPASTE?

ONLY TAKE SHOWERS FOREVER

~OR~

ONLY TAKE BATHS FOREVER?

WOULD YOU RATHER...

HAVE POWER TO CAMOUFLAGE
YOURSELF

~OR~

EAVESDROP FROM ROOMS AWAY?

NEVER EAT MEAT AGAIN

~OR~

EAT ONLY MEAT FOR EVERY MEAL?

SMELL LIKE ROTTEN FISH

~OR~

WEAR SAME CLOTHES EVERY DAY?

WOULD YOU RATHER...

YOUR NOSE GROWS WHEN YOU LIE

~OR~

YOU BURP IN BETWEEN TALKING?

ONE REALLY NICE CHRISTMAS GIFT

~OR~

TEN AVERAGE CHRISTMAS GIFTS?

YOUR FAVORITE NEW TOY

~OR~

24 HRS OF YOUR MOM'S UNDIVIDED
ATTENTION & SNUGGLING?

WOULD YOU RATHER...

GO WILDERNESS CAMPING FOR 1 WEEK

~OR~

HAVE A 1 HOUR SPA MASSAGE?

YOU CAN LISTEN BUT NOT SPEAK

~OR~

YOU CAN SPEAK BUT NOT HEAR?

LISTEN TO A HISSING CAT

~OR~

LISTEN TO A BARKING DOG?

WOULD YOU RATHER...

HAVE A CAT-SIZED ELEPHANT

~OR~

HAVE AN ELEPHANT-SIZED CAT?

STAY OUTSIDE ONLY FOR 1 WEEK

~OR~

BE STUCK INSIDE ONLY FOR 1 WEEK?

HAVE A BUNNY & SNAKE FOR PETS

~OR~

HAVE A BIRD & TARANTULA FOR PETS?

WOULD YOU RATHER...

EAT BROCCOLI FLAVORED ICE CREAM

~OR~

EAT MEAT FLAVORED COOKIES?

HAVE TO SING EVERY WORD

~OR~

GET HICCUPS EVERY 20 MINUTES?

EAT ONE NONPOISONOUS SPIDER

~OR~

HAVE 50 CRAWL ON YOU AT ONCE?

WOULD YOU RATHER...

BE A COMMERCIAL JET PILOT

~OR~

BE A CRUISE SHIP CAPTAIN?

VACATION IN FLORIDA

~OR~

VACATION IN ALASKA?

EAT FROZEN POPS IN WINTER

~OR~

EAT BOWLS OF SOUP IN SUMMER?

WOULD YOU RATHER...

RIDE ON A HOVERCRAFT

~OR~

FLY A DRONE?

EAT A CHOCOLATE COVERED WORM

~OR~

EAT A MINT FLAVORED GRASSHOPPER?

GO APPLE PICKING

~OR~

GO PUMPKIN PICKING?

WOULD YOU RATHER...

GET UNLIMITED DESSERTS

~OR~

GET UNLIMITED ELECTRONICS?

BUILD ANY HOME YOU WANT

~OR~

DRIVE ANY CAR YOU WANT?

HAVE A BACKYARD POOL

~OR~

HAVE A BACKYARD ICE RINK?

WOULD YOU RATHER...

MEET AN ELK IN THE WILD

~OR~

MEET A BUFFALO IN THE WILD?

BE ABLE TO TALK WITH YOUR PET

~OR~

KNOW WHAT YOUR PARENTS ARE THINKING?

HAVE A LARGE FAMILY & NO PETS

~OR~

HAVE A SMALL FAMILY & MANY PETS?

WOULD YOU RATHER...

LIVE IN A TREEHOUSE

~OR~

LIVE IN AN UNDERGROUND HOUSE?

BE A MEDIEVAL KNIGHT

~OR~

BE A WILD WEST COWBOY?

COMPETE IN PRO FOOTBALL

~OR~

COMPETE IN PRO BASKETBALL?

WOULD YOU RATHER...

DRIVE AN EXOTIC SPORTSCAR

~OR~

TAKE EXOTIC VACATIONS?

BE A PRINCESS

~OR~

BE A PIRATE?

BE A MUSIC TEACHER

~OR~

BE A MATH TEACHER?

WOULD YOU RATHER...

BE A POLICE OFFICER

~OR~

BE A FIREFIGHTER?

MEET THE TOOTH FAIRY

~OR~

MEET SANTA CLAUS?

BE A GOOD RUNNER, BAD SWIMMER

~OR~

BE A GOOD SWIMMER, BAD RUNNER?

WOULD YOU RATHER...

BE ABLE TO WRITE CODE

~OR~

BE ABLE TO WRITE A NOVEL?

EAT MEALS WITH NO UTENSILS

~OR~

WASH HANDS WITH NO SOAP?

EAT A WHOLE LEMON

~OR~

EAT A BRUSSEL SPROUT?

WOULD YOU RATHER...

BE A GREAT SPELLER

~OR~

HAVE GREAT HANDWRITING?

DRIVE A BRAND NEW MINIVAN

~OR~

DRIVE A RUSTY OLD SPORTS CAR?

NEVER LOSE ANYTHING AGAIN

~OR~

NEVER BE LATE AGAIN?

WOULD YOU RATHER...

SPEND THE DAY IN GARDENS

~OR~

SPEND THE DAY IN A MUSEUM?

HAVE A BIG HYPER DOG FOR A PET

~OR~

HAVE A SMALL QUIET DOG FOR A PET?

EAT ICE CREAM IN A TACO SHELL

~OR~

EAT NACHOS IN AN ICE CREAM CONE?

WOULD YOU RATHER...

RIDE A TRICYCLE REALLY WELL

~OR~

RIDE AN ADULT BIKE BUT FALL?

LIVE WHERE IT'S VERY HOT & DRY

~OR~

LIVE WHERE IT'S AVERAGE BUT WET?

LIVE WITH COLD WINTERS & SNOW

~OR~

LIVE WITH THREATS OF HURRICANES?

WOULD YOU RATHER...

PLAY PIANO REALLY WELL

~OR~

PLAY GUITAR REALLY WELL?

VISIT AMUSEMENT PARK

~OR~

VISIT WATERPARK?

SWIM NONSTOP LAPS

~OR~

RUN NONSTOP LAPS?

WOULD YOU RATHER...

TAKE A ROAD TRIP TO DESTINATION

~OR~

FLY ON CROWDED AIRPLANE?

EAT PIZZA WITH NO TOPPINGS

~OR~

EAT SPAGHETTI WITH NO SAUCE?

HAVE A PET UNICORN

~OR~

HAVE A PET DRAGON?

WOULD YOU RATHER...

NEVER LEAVE YOUR HOMETOWN

~OR~

NEVER RETURN TO YOUR HOMETOWN?

GIVE YOUR MOM UNLIMITED SPA

~OR~

GIVE YOUR DAD UNLIMITED GOLF?

YOU CAN ONLY SLEEP 2 HRS/NIGHT

~OR~

YOU CAN ONLY EAT 1 MEAL/DAY?

WOULD YOU RATHER...

INSTANTLY LOSE 20 POUNDS

~OR~

INSTANTLY LOSE ALL WRINKLES?

RIDE IN A HELICOPTER

~OR~

PARACHUTE FROM AN AIRPLANE?

MOVE TO ANOTHER COUNTRY

~OR~

MOVE TO ANOTHER CITY?

WOULD YOU RATHER...

HAVE UNCONTROLLED SNEEZING

~OR~

HAVE UNCONTROLLED BURPING?

ONLY WEAR ONE SHOE

~OR~

ONLY WEAR ONE MITTEN?

LIVE WITHOUT ELECTRICITY

~OR~

LIVE WITHOUT RUNNING WATER?

WOULD YOU RATHER...

GET CHICKEN POX YEARLY

~OR~

HAVE BAD ALLERGIES DAILY?

HAVE EVERYTHING TASTE LIKE TACOS

~OR~

NEVER TASTE A TACO AGAIN?

LOSE YOUR FAVORITE KEEPSAKE

~OR~

LOSE YOUR FAVORITE MEMORY?

WOULD YOU RATHER...

GO TRICK-OR-TREATING

~OR~

STAY HOME & HAND OUT CANDY?

HAVE SNOW ALL WINTER

~OR~

HAVE SNOW JUST ON CHRISTMAS?

HAVE A BIG BOAT, CATCH NO FISH

~OR~

HAVE A SMALL BOAT, CATCH MANY FISH?

WOULD YOU RATHER...

VACATION LASTS WHOLE SUMMER

~OR~

SUMMER BREAK IS 3 WKS LONGER?

PAINT BEAUTIFUL PICTURES

~OR~

SING BEAUTIFUL SONGS?

HAVE A MOVIE THEATER AT HOME

~OR~

HAVE A BOWLING ALLEY AT HOME?

WOULD YOU RATHER...

LEARN TO COOK FROM A CHEF

~OR~

LEARN TO DRAW FROM AN ARTIST?

RIDE A SKATEBOARD

~OR~

GO SURFING?

HAVE LOTS OF QUIET NEIGHBORS

~OR~

ONE VERY NOSY NEIGHBOR?

WOULD YOU RATHER...

HUG EVERYONE YOU MEET

~OR~

HIGH FIVE EVERYONE YOU MEET?

OWN EVERY VIDEO GAME

~OR~

OWN EVERY MOVIE DVD?

FEED A GOAT

~OR~

PET A BUNNY?

WOULD YOU RATHER...

OWN YOUR OWN GOLF COURSE

~OR~

OWN YOUR OWN WATERPARK?

DRESS UP LIKE A PIRATE

~OR~

DRESS UP LIKE A NINJA?

ALL FOOD HAS NO CALORIES

~OR~

YOU NEVER GET TIRED?

WOULD YOU RATHER...

BAIT A FISHING HOOK WITH WORMS

~OR~

CLEAN UP CAT HAIRBALLS?

EAT HOT DOG WITH CARAMEL SAUCE

~OR~

DRINK MILK MIXED WITH KETCHUP?

WEAR AN EXPENSIVE WATCH

~OR~

WEAR EXPENSIVE SHOES?

WOULD YOU RATHER...

BE RICH BUT CAN'T SPEND IT

~OR~

BE SMART BUT NOBODY KNOWS?

FLOAT ON A CLOUD

~OR~

SWIM UNDER THE SEA?

BE A HERO TO ONE CHILD

~OR~

BE ADMIRED BY MANY PEOPLE?

WOULD YOU RATHER...

BECOME A BILLIONAIRE

~OR~

CURE A DISEASE?

EAT ONLY FAST FOOD

~OR~

NEVER EAT FAST FOOD AGAIN?

BE GIVEN $100 IN SINGLES

~OR~

BE GIVEN A $100 BILL?

WOULD YOU RATHER...

EVERYONE WANTS YOUR AUTOGRAPH

~OR~

NOBODY KNOWS WHO YOU ARE?

HAVE A SPARE HEART

~OR~

HAVE A SPARE BRAIN?

COLLECT POSTAGE STAMPS

~OR~

COLLECT OLD COINS?

WOULD YOU RATHER...

WAKE UP SUPER EARLY

~OR~

STAY UP SUPER LATE?

GO TO THE GYM EVERY DAY

~OR~

WORKOUT BY YOURSELF DAILY?

SEE THINGS NOBODY ELSE DOES

~OR~

HEAR THINGS NOBODY ELSE DOES?

WOULD YOU RATHER...

NEVER BATHE AGAIN

~OR~

NEVER RUN AGAIN?

BICYCLE ACROSS THE COUNTRY

~OR~

SKATEBOARD ACROSS THE COUNTRY?

HAVE BREAKFAST WITH A CELEBRITY

~OR~

HAVE DINNER WITH THE PRESIDENT

WOULD YOU RATHER...

BE BANNED FROM SOCIAL MEDIA

~OR~

LOSE YOUR TELEPHONE?

GAIN 10 POUNDS

~OR~

HAVE CONSTANT RASHES?

DANCE SOLO ON STAGE

~OR~

GIVE A SPEECH TO A CROWD?

WOULD YOU RATHER...

NEVER BE LATE

~OR~

NEVER LOSE YOUR TEMPER?

BE A BASEBALL PITCHER

~OR~

BE A BASEBALL CATCHER?

BE SHY WITH LOTS OF FRIENDS

~OR~

BE OUTGOING WITH FEW FRIENDS?

WOULD YOU RATHER...

HAVE TEA WITH BRITISH ROYALTY

~OR~

ATTEND A MEXICAN FIESTA?

SLIDE DOWN A RAINBOW

~OR~

SAFELY SEE THE CENTER OF A
TORNADO?

DESIGN A SKYSCRAPER

~OR~

CREATE A HALLOWEEN CORN MAZE?

WOULD YOU RATHER...

MEET DR. SEUSS

~OR~

MEET THE MAD HATTER?

DESIGN A NEW TOY

~OR~

PRODUCE A NEW MOVIE?

SAVE AN ANIMAL FROM EXTINCTION

~OR~

FIND A CURE FOR ALLERGIES?

WOULD YOU RATHER...

USE A TELESCOPE

~OR~

USE A MICROSCOPE?

WAKE UP TO $100 BILL EVERY DAY

~OR~

BE SERVED YOUR 3 FAVORITE MEALS DAILY?

HAVE ENDLESS FOOD IN YOUR FRIDGE

~OR~

HAVE ENDLESS GAS IN YOUR CAR?

WOULD YOU RATHER...

HAVE A PET POLAR BEAR

~OR~

HAVE A PET LEOPARD?

EAT ONE GIANT PANCAKE

~OR~

EAT 100 TINY PANCAKES?

ONLY WEAR BLACK & WHITE

~OR~

ONLY WEAR RAINBOW CLOTHES?

WOULD YOU RATHER...

HAVE A PET PENGUIN

~OR~

HAVE A PET KOMODO DRAGON?

YOUR BACKYARD BE A TRAMPOLINE

~OR~

YOUR BACKYARD BE A WATERPARK?

RIDE A WILD PONY

~OR~

RUN WITH THE BULLS IN SPAIN?

WOULD YOU RATHER...

VISIT AUSTRALIA

~OR~

VISIT CHINA?

MEET YOUR GREAT, GREAT, GREAT, GREAT GRANDMOTHER

~OR~

MEET TEDDY ROOSEVELT?

GO ROLLERSKATING

~OR~

GO BOWLING?

WOULD YOU RATHER...

GO ON AN AFRICAN SAFARI

~OR~

GO ON A SOUTH POLE EXPEDITION?

BE GIVEN $1 MILLION RIGHT NOW

~OR~

BE GIVEN $50K/YR FOR LIFE?

STAY HOME & WATCH A QUIET MOVIE

~OR~

GO OUT TO A LOUD MUSIC CONCERT?

WOULD YOU RATHER...

EAT PANCAKES & BACON

~OR~

EAT WARM OATMEAL W/FRUIT?

BE THE BOSS OF 100 PEOPLE

~OR~

WORK FROM HOME BY YOURSELF?

SPEND A DAY AT THE ZOO

~OR~

SPEND A DAY AT THE PARK?

WOULD YOU RATHER...

HAVE YOUR DREAM JOB

~OR~

BE WEALTHY & DON'T NEED A JOB?

GIVE $1 MILLION TO 1 PERSON

~OR~

GIVE $100K TO 10 PEOPLE?

EAT BIRTHDAY CAKE W/GRAVY

~OR~

EAT A JUICY STEAK WITH FROSTING?

WOULD YOU RATHER...

HAVE YOUR DRAWINGS COME TO LIFE

~OR~

MEET YOUR FAVORITE AUTHOR?

PERFORM ON BROADWAY IN A SMALL ROLE

~OR~

BE THE STAR OF A LOCAL THEATER PRODUCTION?

SPEND 1 DAY BEING A KID AGAIN

~OR~

SPEND 1 DAY 50 YRS IN THE FUTURE?

WOULD YOU RATHER...

READ A FAVORITE BOOK

~OR~

WATCH A FAVORITE MOVIE?

WRESTLE A KANGAROO

~OR~

HUG A KOALA BEAR?

HAVE UNLIMITED CHOCOLATE

~OR~

BE THE FASTEST RUNNER EVER?

WOULD YOU RATHER...

GET A SHOT FROM A DOCTOR

~OR~

HAVE DENTIST FILL A CAVITY?

HAVE 70 DEGREES BUT RAINY

~OR~

HAVE 30 DEGREES BUT SNOWY?

RIDE AN ATV IN THE MOUNTAINS

~OR~

RIDE A SNOWMOBILE ON TRAILS?

WOULD YOU RATHER...

DRINK BANANA FLAVORED MILK

~OR~

CHOCOLATE MILK ?

WRITE A NEWSPAPER COLUMN

~OR~

RECORD A PODCAST?

HAVE 3 HALLOWEENS A YEAR

~OR~

CHRISTMAS LASTS 3 MONTHS?

WOULD YOU RATHER...

EAT BURGERS & ICE CREAM WITH FAMILY

~OR~

FANCY DINNER WITH FRIENDS?

SCALE MOUNT EVEREST

~OR~

TREK THE AMAZON JUNGLE?

WIN THE LOTTERY YOURSELF

~OR~

PICK 3 OTHER PEOPLE TO EACH WIN THE LOTTERY?

WOULD YOU RATHER...

HAVE WINGS

~OR~

HAVE FINS?

WORK 2 DAYS/WK 20 HRS/DAY

~OR~

WORK 5 DAYS/WK 8 HRS/DAY?

EAT BUGS

~OR~

TAKE A BATH IN MUD?

WOULD YOU RATHER...

FIND TRUE LOVE

~OR~

BE SUPER RICH?

DRIVE AN EXPENSIVE SPORTS CAR

~OR~

FLY YOUR OWN PLANE?

SING ALL OF YOUR WORDS

~OR~

SKIP WHILE YOU WALK?

WOULD YOU RATHER...

CREATE HISTORY

~OR~

DELETE IT?

HAVE LEGS AS LONG AS YOUR FINGERS

~OR~

HAVE FINGERS AS LONG AS YOUR LEGS?

EAT A CUP OF DOG FOOD

~OR~

SIX ROTTEN TOMATOES?

WOULD YOU RATHER...

BRUSH YOUR TEETH WITH RANCH DRESSING

~OR~

WASH YOUR FACE WITH MUSTARD?

HAVE WINGS OF A BUTTERFLY

~OR~

THE HORN OF A UNICORN?

HAVE FEET THE SIZE OF A CAR

~OR~

ARMS AS LONG AS A HORSE'S LEG?

Made in the USA
Monee, IL
12 December 2019